FOR ROTEM

DAILY★BARK

SAM THE BEST

TOP DOG WINS IT ALL!

SPORTS
★ ★ #1 SAM! ★ ★
"Stay in School"

GO SAM!

FIRST FIRST FIRST FIRST

S
SAM

1 SAM

SAM SAM SAM

GO SAM!

● ● ○ Printed in four spot colors. ○ ● ●
Designed by Greg Pizzoli and Joann Hill
Hand lettering by Greg Pizzoli
Printed in Malaysia • Reinforced binding
Visit www.disneyhyperionbooks.com

NUMBER ONE SAM

GREG PIZZOLI

Disney · HYPERION BOOKS   New York

Sam was number one.

He was number one in speed.

He was number one at turns.

And he was number one at finishing races in the number-one spot.

So on the day of the big race,
Sam wasn't worried one bit.

He pulled up to the start,
wished "good luck" to his
best friend, Maggie,
revved his engine, and . . .

They were off!

Sam zoomed up to speed,
and nailed all the turns.

He and Maggie were neck-and-neck
as they headed for the finish line,
and then . . .

Sam lost.

Everyone
was cheering
for Maggie!

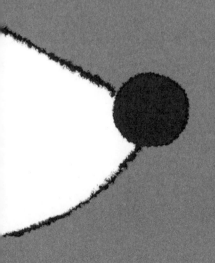

Everyone
except
Sam.

Sam couldn't lose!

He was the best at speed!
He was the best at turns!
He was the best at being
number one!

The night before the next race,
Sam didn't sleep one wink.

At the starting line, Sam was quiet.
The cars lined up.
The engines revved.

Sam didn't say anything to Maggie.

He was too nervous.

In fact, he was so distracted
he missed the starting flag!

Maggie and the other racers had a huge lead, but Sam quickly gained on them.

He was driving his best
and soon passed to the front.

Sam would be number one again!

But then he saw them.

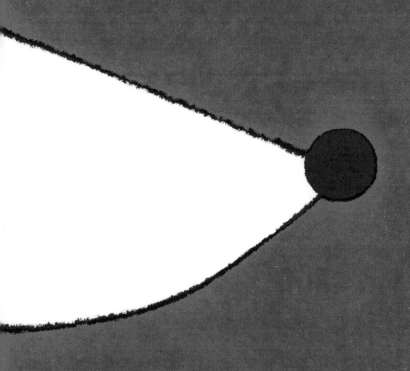

Five chicks crossing the track!

He was headed right for them!

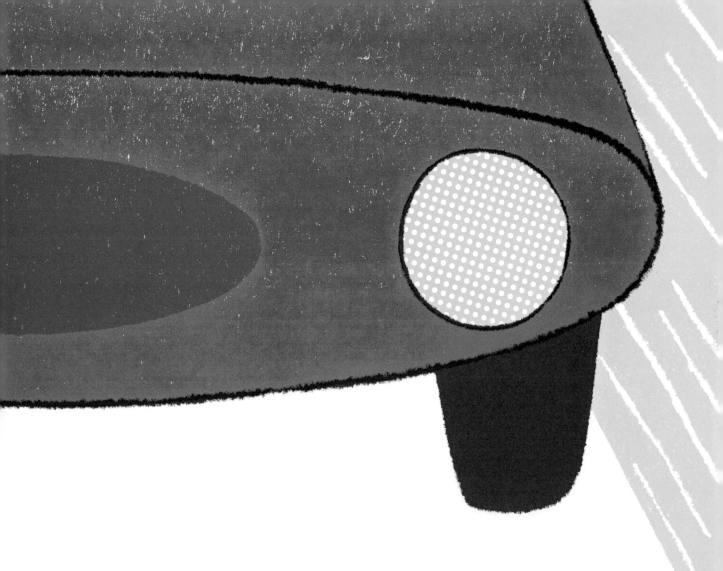

Sam could steer around the chicks, but would the other racers see them in time?

SCREE

Sam slammed on his brakes!

He scurried the chicks to safety
as the other racers flew by.

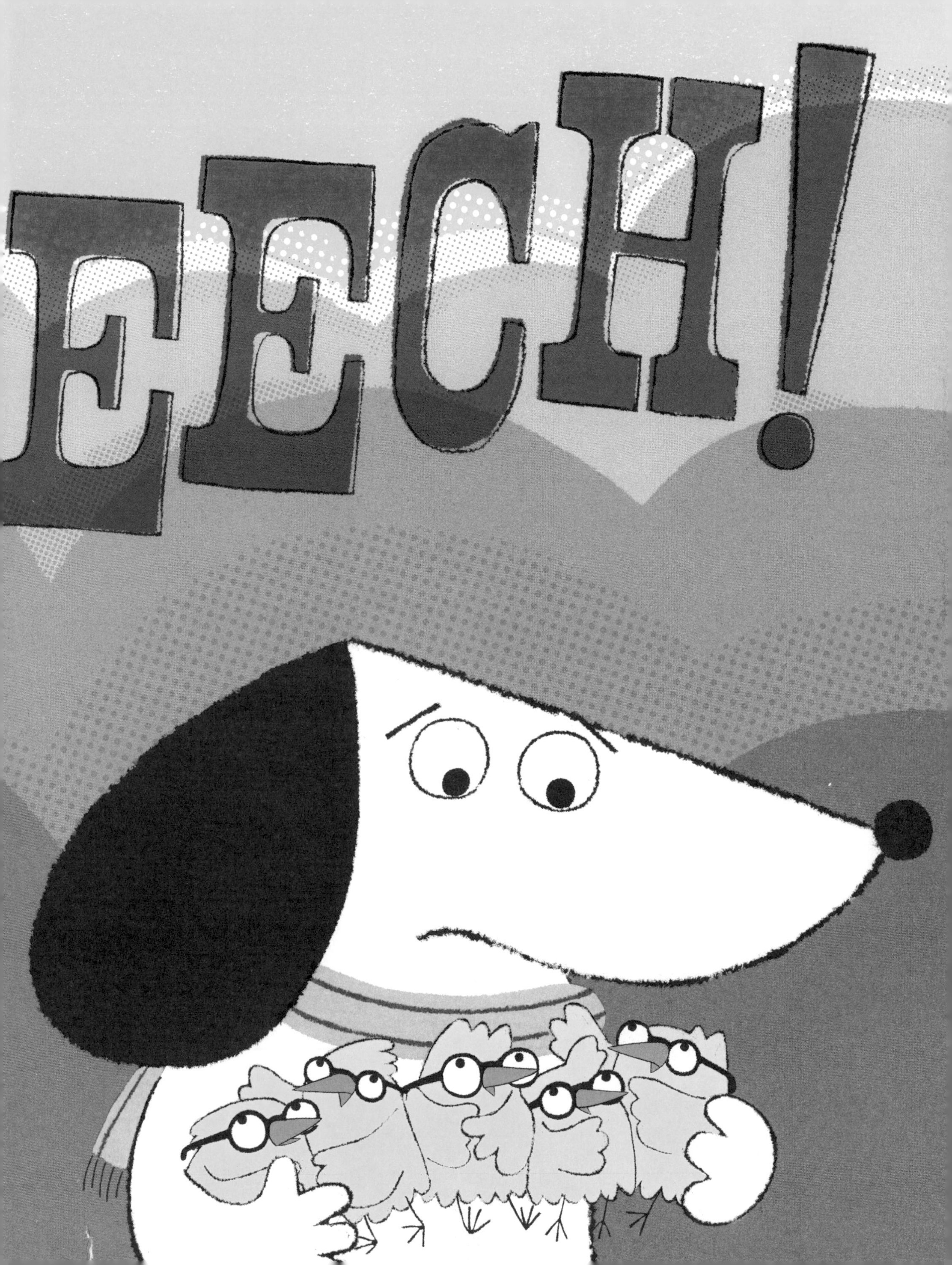
EECH!

Sam finished in last place,
the chicks thanking him the whole way.

Sam was disappointed.

As he approached the finish line, he heard people cheering for the other racers.

But as he got closer, he realized they were cheering for *him*!

And even though he lost another race . . .

His friends still thought
he was number one.

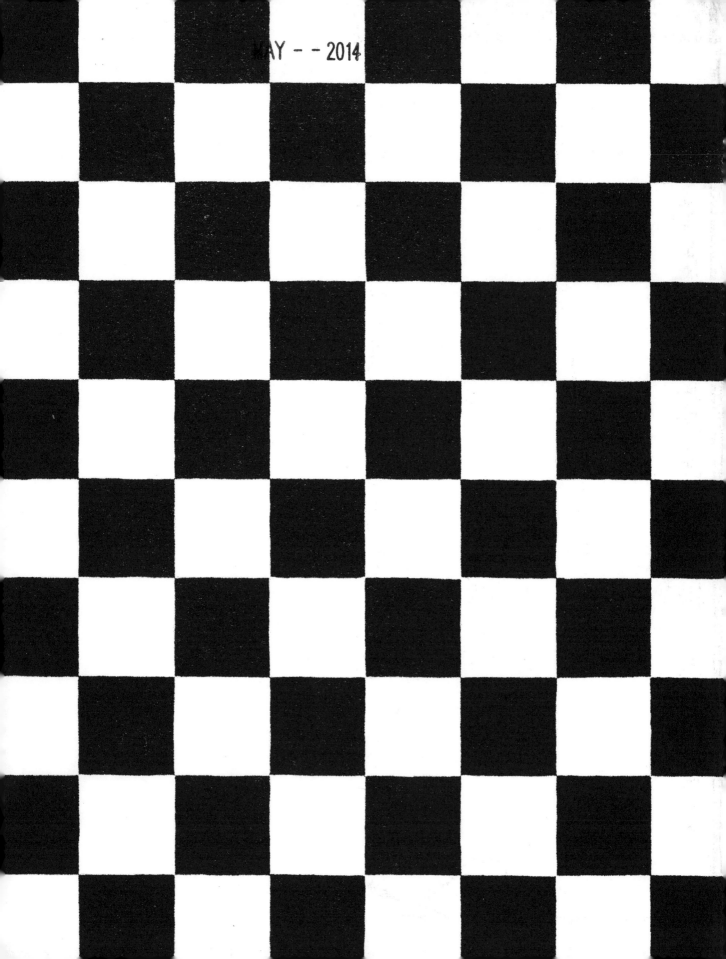